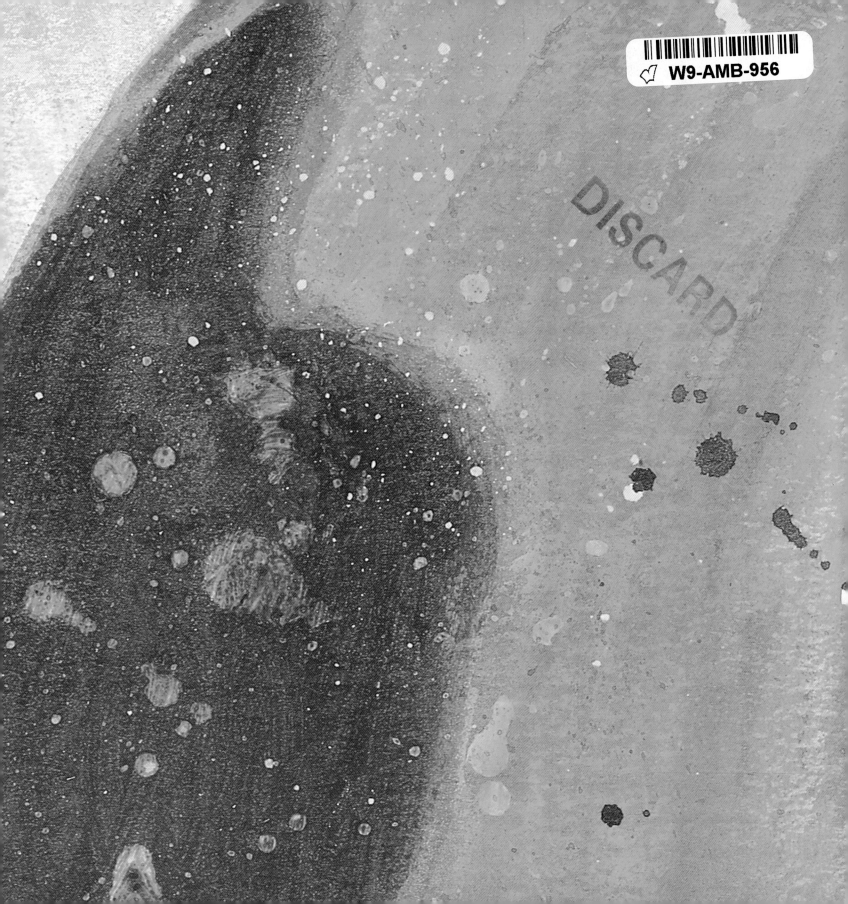

GRRr...

not totally p.c.,
   just **for** P.C. - M.J.
for furry friends everywhere - D.A.

published by the **millbrook press,** inc.,

2 old new milford road, brookfield, ct 06804

devised and produced by the templar company plc,

dorking, surrey, england.

illustration copyright © 1999 by deborah allwright

this edition copyright © 1999 by the templar company plc.

manufactured in china

all rights reserved.

design by mike jolley, words "tweaked" by dugald **steer,**
the "BOOM" pop by richard **hawke.**

Library of Congress Cataloging-in-Publication Data

Jolley, Mike.
     Grunter, a pig with an attitude!/ words by Mike Jolley;
pictures by Deborah Allwright.
          p.   cm.
     Summary: Grunter, a pig with an obnoxious attitude, gets an
explosive surprise from the other farmyard animals on his birthday.
     ISBN 0-7613-1308-7 (lib. bdg.). -- ISBN 0-7613-0449-5 (trade: hc)
     [1. Pigs--Fiction.   2. Domestic animals--Fiction.   3. Behavior--Fiction.
4. Birthdays--Fiction.]   I. Allwright, Deborah, ill. II. Title.
PZ7.J66245Gr 1999
[E]--dc21   98-35832
                                                           CIP
                                                           AC

5 4 3 2 1

(we have liftoff!)

GRUNTER

attitude!

a pig with an

words by
mike jolley

pictures by
deborah allwright

the **millbrook press**
brookfield, connecticut

This is the story

of a small green farm

with a large

pink problem.

This is the small green farm...

This is **Gregory,** but he is known
as GRUNTER, because that's what he does!

He **hates** everything...

...and everyone.

← last flower for **3** miles

He is overfed...

...and overweight.

He is mad,

bad,

angry

and **sad.**

(And dangerous to know on any day with a **d** in it).

He has a **bad** attitude...

...and even **worse** gas!

Yesterday,

he flattened the farmer,

spat on the cat,

dunked the dog,

batted the bull

and **mashed**

three near-sighted mice

into the mud.

The day before, he rammed the rooster, grabbed the goat and **choked** the chicks with one of his outbursts. He ran **amok** in the **muck,** sat on the sheep and dropped something **dirty** on the **duck!**

The other animals think that he is **too big**

for his britches.

The other animals **think** that he should be taught a lesson.

Today is GRunTeR's birthday

and he is all alone!

No one has remembered...

...or have they?

This is the small green farm...

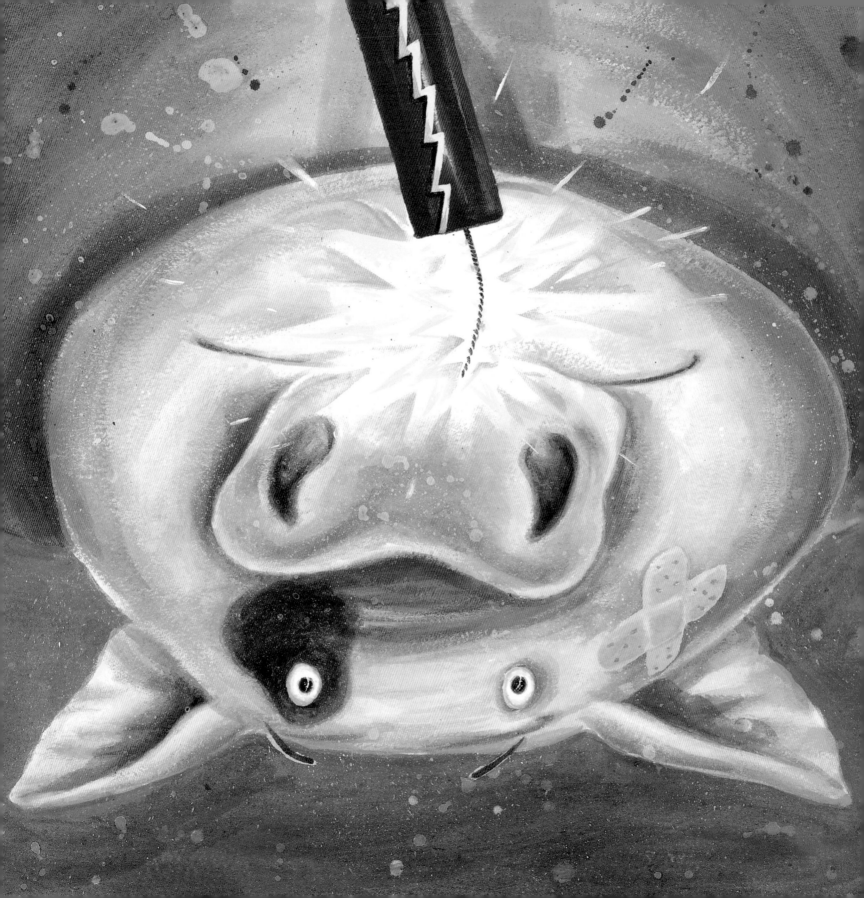

...this **was** the problem!

But what goes up **must** come down.

(To be continued?)